VALENTINO THE LOVE BUNNY

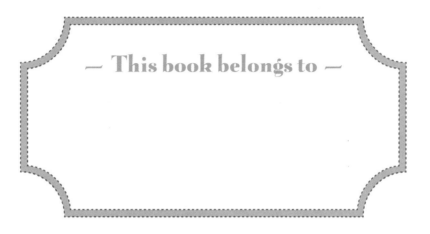

— This book belongs to —

...AND HOW HE CAME TO BE

Book One

This book is dedicated to my beloved mother,
Beatrice "Bibi" Fairbanks. Our dream came true.

— ∞ —

"All that I am, or ever hope to be, I owe to my angel mother."

— **Abraham Lincoln**

Valentino
The Love Bunny

By

MARGARITA FAIRBANKS
ILLUSTRATIONS BY SUZAN DUVAL

...AND HOW HE CAME TO BE

Book One

VALENTINO THE LOVE BUNNY, LLC

The sun drifted lazily across the sky, signaling the end of another perfect afternoon at the little pet shop by the sea. What made this place so special was that the animals lived side by side, and except for those that were too small and delicate, they roamed freely within the shop. There was George, the beautiful Serama rooster, Kip the grey kitty, who never shied from customers and was always the first to say "hello," and Houdini, the chameleon, who could be found lounging on a limb. There was also a newcomer — a little white rabbit with black ears, a black heart around one eye and another on his cheek.

The animals were happy together here, and even though they were different SPECIES, they shared one very powerful bond. They were all waiting to find their forever homes! George fancied himself the one in charge and had spent most of the afternoon perched on the bunny enclosure. He had gone out of his way to make their new friend feel welcome, knowing the little bunny might feel lonely in this unfamiliar place. The only thing that broke the steady harmony was the chime of bells as the shop door opened and closed. At this sound all the animals would come to attention, waiting to see who had entered and what it might mean, and the bells were chiming now.

"Hello," said the shopkeeper to the lady entering the store, "how is my dear Animal Lady?" They had known each other for a long time, as the Animal Lady was a frequent visitor to the shop. "I was hoping you would come in!" said the shopkeeper. She knew that the Animal Lady had long dreamed of adding a bunny to her family and could hardly contain her excitement as they turned toward the small pet enclosure. "There is someone very special I want you to meet. George has been keeping an eye on him the last couple days, but I think maybe he has been waiting for you..."

The Animal Lady smiled radiantly upon her first glimpse at the sweet black and white bunny. "Hello little one!" she said to the bunny as his eyes turned to face her and he raised himself up onto his back legs to get a closer sniff. "There is something special about this bunny," the shopkeeper said, "even Kip thinks so!" Kip the kitty ran his body through the Animal Lady's legs, mcowing as if in agreement, while George clucked protectively.

"May I hold him?" asked the Animal Lady. "Of course, but be careful of his claws. Bunnies can kick if they are frightened." The shopkeeper helped her to gently pick up this tiny baby with the mark of love around his eye. She closed her eyes and what she felt in her hands was pure LOVE, soft and warm; a feeling of complete and total peace. The bunny gently sniffed at the Animal Lady's fingers and gave a little lick-kiss to her thumb. "What a love bunny!" exclaimed the Animal Lady, and in that instant she knew that this was the very bunny she had been dreaming of.

"Do you believe in DESTINY?" she asked the shopkeeper, "that something is meant to be? This bunny has to come home with me. He absolutely must!" The Animal Lady gently put the bunny down and wiped away a tear of joy that had fallen from her eye.

Excitement filled the air. The little bunny had found a forever home! The shopkeeper helped the Animal Lady gather up all the supplies she would need for her new bunny's care: hay and bunny pellets for food, a fleece pillow and blanket to make a cozy bed, litter and a litter box for a bunny potty, and a "bunny condo" to put all these things in. The other animals watched all the commotion, knowing that soon they would have to say good-bye to their little friend. The bunny looked fondly at the other animals as he was placed inside a small carrier. "Goodbye friends," he sighed softly, as the Animal Lady gathered her bags of supplies in one hand and the bunny in the other. The chiming of the bells on the door was heard once more, and the little pet shop by the sea bid farewell to the little white fur ball with black ears and black hearts on his face.

The Animal Lady put the bunny into her car where another member of the family, Sparky, a little chihuahua-terrier mix, was peacefully napping on the back seat. He was roused as the bunny's carrier was placed next to him, and yawning loudly, he turned to give a sleepy sniff at the little black and white rabbit inside. The bunny felt shy, but was curious to know who this was. "Hello, it's nice to meet you Mr. Dog." Sparky yawned again, and wagged his tail. "Hi there, my name is Sparky. Are you coming home with us?" "I am! What is home like?" the bunny asked enthusiastically. "It's wonderful!" said Sparky between yawns, then added "for now, I think maybe we should nap." Sparky didn't want to be rude, but the rocking of the moving car was sending him back to sleep. "HOME," he mumbled, "HOME SWEET HOME..."

Sparky was asleep again and dreaming of his own journey home. It was only a few months before. He didn't remember a lot of his puppy days, but he did remember wandering alone, lost in the nearby hills. He was so scared, but he kept walking and barking to keep his spirits up. Thankfully, someone heard him and took him to a local pet shelter. It was there that he met the Animal Lady who, after one look at him, said, "This was meant to be! You absolutely must come home with me!" Sparky sighed happily as he slept.

The late afternoon sunlight warmed the bunny as the car drove on, but he was too excited to nap. He imagined what home would look like and who else he might meet. He also thought about his friends at the pet shop that had been left behind. Would they find a home too? With someone like the Animal Lady? When she held him in her hands, he felt a wave of happy energy flow from her, which made him feel happy and safe. He wasn't sure what caused that good feeling, but kissing her hand felt like the right thing to do in return. His bunny instincts told him that he could TRUST and love this person, even though they had just met.

In no time they arrived at their final destination, Home Sweet Home. When the door opened, the trio were greeted by two big, black, fluffy standard poodles — a father and son — named Miro and Lucca. The two dogs jumped with excitement as they could smell the arrival of someone new. It was unlike anything they had ever smelled! "Who is in the box?" they yelped at one another. "Quiet down boys, calm down, it's time to be gentle," said the Animal Lady. As soon as the two dogs settled down, she took the little bunny out of his carrier and placed him on the floor, inviting first Miro then Lucca to come and say hello.

Sniff, sniff, sniff, a new member of the family had arrived! The little bunny again felt shy. These dogs were much bigger than he was. Their noses tickled his whiskers and fur as they smelled his little face, and the bunny decided it would be best to hold as still as possible. "Hello there, it's nice to meet you Mr. Dog and Mr. Dog." The little bunny was anxious to make a good first impression. "What a very POLITE bunny you are. Welcome to the family. I'm Miro and this is my son, Lucca. What is your name?" The little bunny didn't know what to say. He didn't have a name. He looked up at Miro who immediately understood. "Don't worry little one, the Animal Lady will sort you out," said Miro lovingly, and to make the bunny feel more welcome he gave him a few grooming licks. This took the bunny by surprise and made him instantly recall the happy memory of the grooming licks he had received from his own mother that calmed him and made him feel loved. The bunny now knew that he had been accepted and was truly a part of this family.

Miro and the bunny turned and gazed at the Animal Lady who had been giving it quite a bit of thought. It was clear from the start that the bunny's appearance would have a lot to do with his name. It's not very common to be born with a beautiful black heart around one eye! She looked at his sweet face and the first thing that came to her mind was... Valentine! Valentine? Somehow that didn't sound just right. She looked at him again and thought, Valentino! That sounded so much nicer, and it was a name associated with love, which fit perfectly with his heart markings. That was it! "Valentino The Love Bunny because you are such a loving bunny! What do you think?" The Animal Lady picked up the little bunny and stroked him gently between his ears. He nuzzled her cheek then turned to Miro and Lucca and said "My name is Valentino, The Love Bunny!"

Now, **Valentino didn't** know this, but he had not yet met all the members of his new family. It wouldn't do to bring a new family member home and not make all the proper introductions, so the Animal Lady put Valentino into his carrier and walked him over to a nearby barn. Valentino could smell dirt, straw and wood shavings and saw a new animal that he had never seen before. The Animal Lady took him out of his crate and the next thing he knew, he was nose to nose with a horse. Horses have big nostrils and the strong flow of air coming in and out of those nostrils was hot, like a warm breeze right in Valentino's face. You might certainly have thought that Valentino would be afraid, but no, he was not afraid, he was interested in this beautiful animal. Horses and rabbits have an excellent sense of smell and these two were busy getting to know each other through their noses.

"Welcome to the family little one, my name is Pandereto," said the horse. "I'm Valentino The Love Bunny, it's very nice to meet you" replied Valentino, who instantly took a liking to his new brother. They continued to sniff one another when Valentino said, "I smell hay, is that what you eat?" "Yes," said Pandereto, "and you smell like hay, too, is that what you eat?" "Yes, I love hay, so I guess we have more in common than we could have imagined!" Pandereto gathered a mouthful of hay from his feeding bin and shared a snack with the newest member of the family.

After a short visit the Animal Lady took Valentino back inside. She set up his bunny condo and prepared his first dinner. Rabbits are vegetarians, which means they don't eat meat, chicken or fish. The main food in their diet is hay, but they also need fresh vegetables every day. Valentino hopped happily to his food tray where a feast of organic kale, parsley, dandelion greens, cilantro and dill was waiting for him. Valentino ate his greens and a little hay then washed it all down with some cool, clear water. Valentino felt so content. He started thinking of what a big day it had been. Sparky was right, home was wonderful! Valentino loved his new family with all his heart. He curled up in his new bed, sighed dreamily, and within moments was fast asleep.

The days passed quickly in Valentino's world and soon he was no longer a baby bunny. That's not to say that he still wasn't very small, but he was now big enough to wander by himself in the house and garden. Valentino spent most of his day playing and having fun. He had lots of toys that kept him busy and many that he loved to chew: a pinecone, a toy carrot, a willow basket and even the odd bit of furniture here and there (although the Animal Lady didn't like that so much.) All that chewing helped to keep Valentino's teeth from growing too long, because rabbit teeth continue to grow throughout their life. Hay is the most important food in a rabbit's diet because it has lots of important nutrients, but also because it has a lot of fiber. Chewing through the tough grass helped to keep Valentino's teeth the perfect size.

Valentino's favorite meal of the day was breakfast. This was the time when he would enjoy a small bowl of the yummiest fresh fruit of the season, diced just the right size for his little mouth. Mmm, bananas, the best, then papaya, which was so good for his digestion and made him smell sweet! Blueberries, apples, cherries and pears; white peaches, when they were in season, were his favorite treat of all! After every meal he licked his tiny little lips with his tiny pink tongue. Valentino was learning how necessary a good diet was and that all the organic fruit and vegetables he ate gave him great energy through the day. He wondered what meal time must be like for the rabbits that lived in the wilderness that had to forage for every bite. They did not have the comforts and the ease of life that he had. Valentino knew that he was one lucky bunny, and he was GRATEFUL for everything.

t would be fair to say that Valentino was a very good bunny, but there was one time of day when he was naughty, and that was bedtime. It was perfectly understandable in his opinion. Valentino was able to play freely throughout the day in his home and garden and even though he loved his bunny condo, he did not want his freedom or his fun to end. Valentino was so sensitive that he knew his eight o'clock bedtime was coming even before the clock struck. He always knew! Before the Animal Lady even had a chance to say, "Time for bed boys," he would begin a nightly game of chase. Valentino would run first under the living room couch, then under the dining table, back under the couch, into the bedroom under the bed, back to the living room under the couch, again under the dining table, all to keep from going to bed!

 Valentino was a fast runner, but this was one game the Animal Lady always won. Sometimes she needed help, but Valentino always ended up in her loving arms. His little heart would be racing from all this activity and the Animal Lady worried that he would overexert himself. Rabbits are very delicate, so they have to be treated carefully, gently and most of all, calmly. The Animal Lady followed these rules, but bedtime was bedtime and she had to be firm. Besides, every time Valentino was scooped up in her arms, he also got smothered with kisses and this felt good, very good. Yes, it was fun to play chase, but once he was in his soft, warm, cozy bed, he would settle in happily for the night.

Valentino adapted well to life with his new family. He had four new brothers — three dogs and a horse — a loving human family, which included the Animal Lady, her husband, their children and their grand-children, fifteen in all. He especially loved the babies aged two, three, four, and five, who had by now given him many names, the most common being *Tino,* but they called him *Tiny* and *Teenerton* as well. In fact, you could often hear a little voice shriek, "It's Tino time!" These nicknames made him feel special, as did they. He knew he was part of something important, a FAMILY filled with love.

He had a beautiful place to live full of wonder. His garden was like a jungle, bursting with color and life. There were flowers, plants and trees of all shapes and sizes that were also home to froggies, birds and bees. Yes, he thought, he was truly on top of the world, still, Valentino had feelings inside himself he couldn't make sense of. He felt there was more to life than just having fun. He wanted to have a PURPOSE, a way to share the happiness he felt everyday.

As he lay pensively on the cool grass in the shade of some brilliant irises, he asked his froggie friends, "Why am I so lucky? Why am I so blessed?" The froggies were moved by this unusual looking bunny with hearts so clearly marking his eye and cheek and tried to help. "Well, have you ever looked at yourself in a mirror?" asked one of the frogs. "A mirror?" said Valentino, "what answers will I find there?" "A mirror," said the other frog, "will show you what you look like. Maybe if you could see yourself, you might find an answer in what you see." "Oh," said Valentino, "thank you, I'll give it a try," and he knew then and there that the next thing he had to do was find a mirror.

Valentino rushed back inside the house where he found Sparky in the living room looking somewhat anxious. "Is everything alright, Sparky?" asked Valentino. "I accidentally knocked over a flower vase," answered Sparky, "and I'm afraid the Animal Lady is going to be angry with me." "I can see that you're worried, but you shouldn't be," said Valentino, "the Animal Lady loves you more than some vase and besides, accidents happen! Anyway, you know how I like to nibble on the wooden baseboards and the Animal Lady has never gotten upset at me." And this was true, because the Animal Lady understood that this was part of a bunny's NATURE, that chewing is what bunnies need to do. Sparky felt reassured. "Thank you, Valentino, you really know how to make a pup feel better." Sparky thought that Valentino had a special way of giving love and was glad to have him as a brother.

Feeling that Sparky was at ease, Valentino now turned his full attention to the beautiful antique mirror next to one of his favorite nibbling spots. It wasn't as if he hadn't seen the mirror, he had just never given it much thought. Now he gave it a good long look and contemplated his reflection in it. Soon enough, he focused on two things in particular: the heart shapes on his face. "Hmm," he said to himself, "I wonder why I have these two hearts on my face. I have never seen hearts like these on anyone else." This was curious indeed, but the more he thought about it, the more he thought it was no accident. The froggies had said he might find the answer to his questions in the mirror, and when he looked at these hearts, he somehow felt they were related to finding his purpose. Those hearts are a sign of LOVE, he thought, and my name is Valentino The Love Bunny. Valentino knew he had found a powerful clue that left him with a lot to think about.

Valentino was deep in thought when he heard the door open and the Animal Lady entered the room. The moment he saw her, he could sense that something was wrong. "Tino, come here, Teenie." She sat on the floor next to him and waited for him to approach. Valentino hopped onto her crossed legs and was gently lifted into a warm embrace. Valentino could feel the Animal Lady's heart beating quickly, but as he nuzzled her, he felt it slow down. He sensed that he brought comfort with his softness, stillness and warmth, and though Valentino was not yet sure of his purpose, the Animal Lady certainly was. She knew that anytime she felt sad, anxious or upset, she could just hold Valentino close in a little special nook that was just for him. She placed him under her neck, next to her cheek and over her heart, and very quickly she would feel happy again. That feeling of love spread through her and dissolved any sadness she had.

As Valentino lay nestled in the comfort of the Animal Lady's arms, he listened to her coo, "You ARE The Love Bunny, Valentino, you ARE The Love Bunny." Slowly, the pieces to his puzzle began to fit together. He reflected upon his journey and recalled all the love and kisses he received, not just at bedtime, but all the time, and not just from the Animal Lady, but from all his family. He thought about the hearts on his face and his special name. That's it! Valentino realized he had the ability to make others feel LOVE. Now he understood without a shadow of a doubt that spreading LOVE was his purpose. Little did Valentino know his life was about to unfold into a great adventure, however, he was sure of one thing — his purpose was to spread LOVE all along the way...

The words in this glossary are commonly used in day to day life. We think we know what they mean, but do we really? In Valentino's world, these words define his life and are also what make us uniquely human. Valentino believes they are important words for people to live by to make the world a better place.

SPECIES · A group of something that shares the same physical features and traits. Valentino is a member of the rabbit species, characterized by very soft fur, long whiskers and ears, strong hind legs and a short fluffy tail.

PURPOSE · The reason for which someone or something exists. Valentino's purpose is to spread love everywhere he goes.

GRATEFUL/GRATITUDE · The state of being thankful. To recognize when someone or something brings goodness, joy or benefit to your life and you express thanks. Valentino felt grateful for the loving family he had found.

HOME · A place where you live and feel safe, happy and at peace. When Valentino met his new family, he knew he was home.

HOME SWEET HOME · A saying that describes that home is the place you like more than any other. In the car, Valentino heard Sparky, the Terrier, mumble "HOME, HOME SWEET HOME," as he drifted off to sleep.

LOVE · A deep, abiding affection for family, friends and animals, that creates feelings of happiness, tenderness and warmth. Also an expression of concern and charity for others. Love is at the heart of Valentino's life.

FAMILY · A group that forms a household and can be related by blood or bonded by friendship. Members of a family trust and care for one another and are always there for each other. Valentino's family consists of humans and animals of different species.

DESTINY · An unknown force that takes your life in a direction that appears as if it is supposed to happen. The minute the Animal Lady held Valentino, she knew it was their destiny to be together.

TRUST · To believe in someone and be confident that you can rely on them for anything at any time. When the Animal Lady held Valentino, his instincts told him he could trust and love her.

POLITE · A respectful way of showing courtesy, good manners and thoughtfulness for others. Miro the Poodle appreciated what a very polite bunny Valentino was at their first meeting.

NATURE · Qualities in people or animals that are not by choice; they exist as an essential and permanent part of their being. The Animal Lady understood that chewing was part of a bunny's nature, something Valentino needed to do to keep his teeth healthy.

OM · A sacred word and sound used in the Hindu religion for chanting and meditation, which is a form of self-reflection. Om is said to be the sound of the universe. "The Animal Lady closed her eyes and what she felt was pure LOVE... a feeling of complete and total peace." (The Om symbol is pictured at the top of this page, see if you can find it on page 3!)

Clockwise from the left: Lucca, Valentino, Margarita, Miro and Sparky.

Afterword

Hello, my name is Margarita and I have adored animals my whole life. "The Animal Lady" character in this book is based on the real-life adventures I have with my bunny named Valentino, and our animal family. I was exceptionally blessed to have a mother who recognized, understood and nurtured my passion for animals, which defines a large part of who I am today and why I relate to animals as I do. Some of my greatest memories are of bringing home lost pets, and instead of being told "NO," I was told "YES!" This brought with it such affirmation and a sense of well-being that has followed me my entire life. When I think of how many children may have brought home a stray kitten and been told NO, a puppy and told NO, a FISH and told NO, NO, NO... it brings tears to my eyes. Animals, and especially pets, are a gift from God. Animals live in the moment and are loyal beyond words. They are pure love and they are healing which is why there are so many animal groups that minister to the sick, the elderly and the suffering.

I have always had cats and dogs, and today I have three dogs named Miro, Lucca and Sparky. I also have a beautiful horse called Pandereto, which means "Tambourine" in Spanish. However, I always wanted a bunny. I also had a beta fish named "Poisson," which means "fish" in French. When he died, I was heartbroken. I went to the pet shop to see about finding a new fish, and it was there that I laid eyes on Valentino for the first time. If ever there was destiny, then this was it! The minute I held him, I knew we were meant for each other. I felt a sense of peace and Valentino let me know he felt the same way by gently licking my finger.

Rabbits are such interesting animals. The first thing I noticed without really understanding this species, is that one must approach them on their terms. In other words, "Think and act like a rabbit!" They are a very sensitive animal and their nature first and foremost is to survive. They have an excellent sense of smell and panoramic vision, allowing them to see everything behind as well as in front of them. They react to the slightest stimuli and are aware of absolutely everything. Anxiety is particularly contagious to rabbits, meaning you have to be calm — and herein lies the beauty of this relationship. It forces one to be peaceful and quiet regardless of anything else. I started noticing my pattern of turning to Valentino when upset, and knowing I had to be calm for him, made me calm for ME! I also noticed that when other people encountered him, they were warmed by his presence and driven by curiosity to stroke his soft fur. So, I started imagining how I could make this bunny a comfort for others as well, and that's how the *Valentino The Love Bunny* book series came to be.

If you are thinking about getting a rabbit as a pet, keep in mind that this is an animal that needs specialized care and attention. If you provide your bunny with all the things they need, you will be rewarded with an amazing companion that will provide you with abiding love.

Visit **www.valentinothelovebunny.com** for more bunny tips, information on the real-life Valentino and updates on upcoming books.

About the Illustrator

SUZAN DUVAL is a self-taught artist who was born and raised in a 5th generation Southern California family.

She always enjoyed sketching animals and flowers, and during the time she raised her two children, this was a preferred family pastime. Her art evolved into tile painting, creating faux finishes, wall murals, and architectural renderings. After a debilitating injury on her right wrist, she used her painting skills to strengthen her hand, and in the process, produced many works of art.

While assisting as a caregiver for author Margarita Fairbanks' mother, Bibi, Suzan was introduced to the real-life Valentino. She connected to his unique qualities and fell in love with the mission he represented. Margarita immediately recognized that Suzan was destined to breathe life and personality into the Valentino character and *The Love Bunny* book series. As Suzan puts it, "It's not just a job, it's a calling and I'm honored to be creating illustrations for his many adventures."

Suzan resides in Santa Barbara, California.

Valentino's adventures will begin in Book 2:

VALENTINO THE LOVE BUNNY
TAKES FLIGHT!

Available 2015

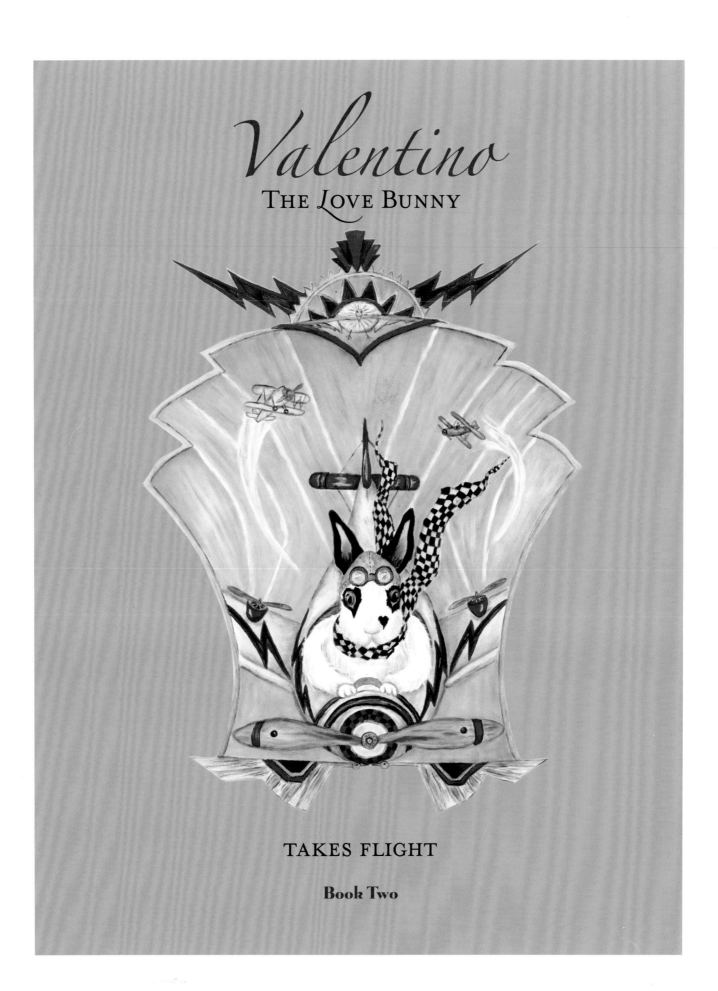

Valentino
The Love Bunny

TAKES FLIGHT

Book Two

Special thanks to my daughter and contributing author, Jessica Bradshaw

This book was art directed by Margarita Fairbanks, designed by Ruth Von Eberstein and edited by Sarah Ettman-Sterner. The fine art illustrations by Suzan Duval were created using layered washes of oil paint on gesso board. The text was set in 14-point "Mrs. Eaves" Roman, designed by Zuzana Licko in 1996. A revival of Baskerville font, named after Sarah Eaves, John Baskerville's housekeeper, who later became his wife. John Baskerville, a printer and typographer in the mid-18th century, designed Baskerville font in 1923. This book was printed and bound at Haagen Printing, Typecraft Inc., in Santa Barbara, California. The production was supervised by Janie Arnold and Scott Gordon.

— ∞ —